T0353845

NORMAN THE NEWT
in
'Wow!'

By
T.N. CRAWFORD

AuthorHouse™ UK
1663 Liberty Drive
Bloomington, IN 47403 USA
www.authorhouse.co.uk
UK TFN: 0800 0148641 (Toll Free inside the UK)
UK Local: 02036 956322 (+44 20 3695 6322 from outside the UK)

Because of the dynamic nature of the Internet, any web addresses or links contained in this book may have changed
since publication and may no longer be valid. The views expressed in this work are solely those of the author and do
not necessarily reflect the views of the publisher, and the publisher hereby disclaims any responsibility for them.

Any people depicted in stock imagery provided by Getty Images are models,
and such images are being used for illustrative purposes only.
Certain stock imagery © Getty Images.

This book is printed on acid-free paper.

ISBN: 979-8-8230-8848-0 (sc)
ISBN: 979-8-8230-8850-3 (hc)
ISBN: 979-8-8230-8849-7 (e)

Library of Congress Control Number: 2024912570

Print information available on the last page.

Published by AuthorHouse 06/26/2024

authorHOUSE

'Twixt Cotter's Approach and Narrow Dale,
is a charming hamlet with a tale,
through trees, you can just see,
hidden and secretly,
lies a bubbling pool, on the trail.

Down came a thirsty squadron of bees,
to this small oasis, fringed with trees,
with great care, gently done,
newts lay eggs, one by one,
beneath the reeds, rattling in the breeze.

Clambering and splashing, frogs jumps in,
croaking away, creating a din,
with frogs, it's a riot,
but the newts are quiet,
as the pond water begins to spin.

Under the lily-pads, down below,
with lots of changes to undergo,
as newt eggs are hatching,
they are quite eye-catching,
one special 'newtling', begins to grow!

This is a story of a newt that's green,
Norman's his name and he's seldom seen,
with an enormous splash,
he'd be gone in a flash,
leaving bubbles to show where he'd been!

Who can keep up with this nippy newt?
swishing his tail, through the pond, he'd shoot,
games of tag, he would play,
with the fish, every day,
one moment chased, the next in pursuit!

For Norman takes it all in his stride,
bugs can't swim, so he gives them a ride,
without him, they would drown,
with a smile, not a frown,
helping them, it fills Norman with pride.

Norman's skin got tighter, as he grew,
taking it off, was seen by few,
not hurting him, to peel,
and it's better to feel,
off with the old and on with the new!

Norman the newt would never have guessed,
bright orange with black dots on his chest,
he went from green to grey,
down his back, all the way,
was a stunning magnificent crest!

This year is over – it's been a blast,
and for Norman, the time has gone fast,
with the first flake of snow,
he really has to go,
for this Summer, is far from his last!

20

SPRING SUMMER SLEEP

When the season ends, Norman takes care,
with fun and food, he has had his share,
unaware, fast asleep,
with not even a peep,
until Spring, by the pond, he'll be there!

Printed in the United States
by Baker & Taylor Publisher Services

ISBN 979-8-8230-8848-0

51318

9 798823 088480

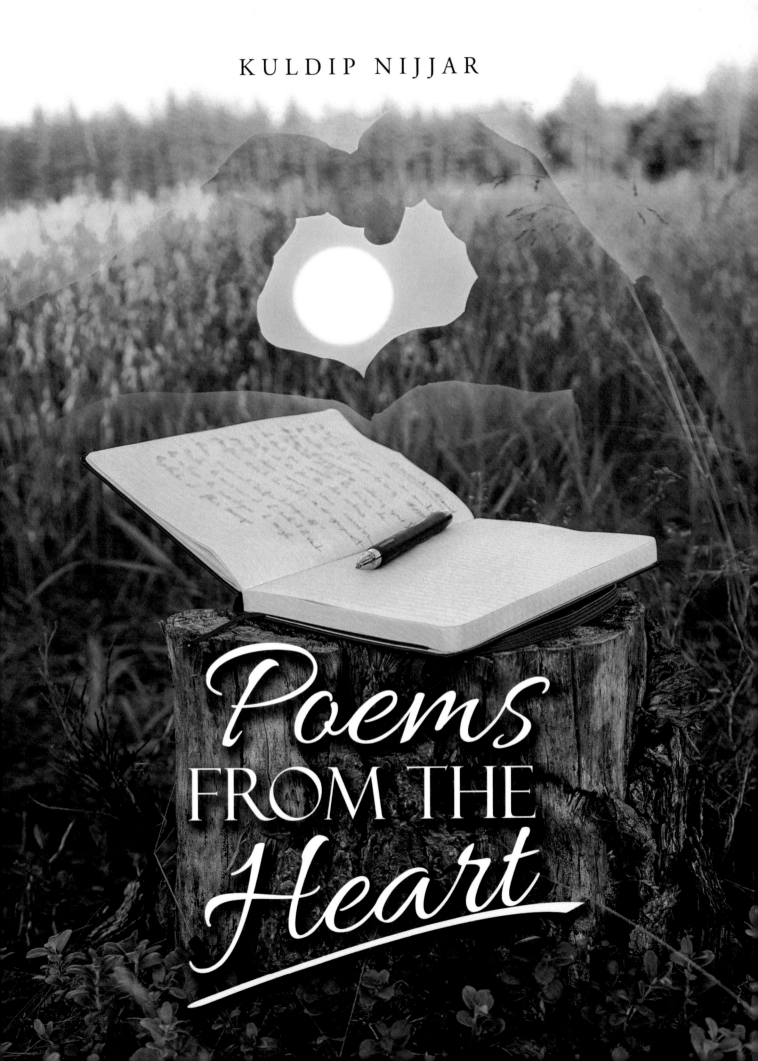

KULDIP NIJJAR

Poems
FROM THE
Heart